DEATHWOOD DAMIAN
STRIKES AGAIN!

Good spellers please note: these letters have been reproduced exactly as written.

Deathwood Damian
STRIKES AGAIN!

Hazel Townson

Illustrated by Tony Ross

ANDERSEN PRESS • LONDON

For Cathy, my lovely caring daughter, with thanks for everything.

First published in 2008 by
Andersen Press Limited,
20 Vauxhall Bridge Road, London SWlV 2SA

British Library Cataloguing in Publication Data available

ISBN 978 184270 707 4

Batch the First

99 Beach Prospect,
Walsea

4th August

Dear Damian Drake,

I don't usually write to boys out of the blue but I saw you in that play at WADS (Walsea Amateurs). I didn't really want to go to it; I hate circuses and thought 'Balls Up' was a cringe-making title. But my big brother Colin was in it – he was the clown with the purple nose – and he made us all go, my mum, my auntie Velda, our Suzie and me. Only our dad had a lucky escape as he's away, detained at Her Majesty's pleasure.

I didn't hear much of the play as our Suzie was crunching crisps all the time and banging her feet on the seat in front, she's only four and doesn't know any better but she's a pest to sit next to. Still, I thought your juggling bit went well. Even when the blue ball flew out over the stalls it just looked like part of the play. In fact, when it hit my auntie Velda on the head and she gave that bloodcurdling shriek some people thought she'd been specially planted in the audience.

Our Colin tells me your dad is a multibillionaire as well as a Sir, and you live at that posh Deathwood Hall which is only up the road from where we live, I always peer through the gates when I go past. Mrs Crabbe, our English teacher, is always wittering on about how we should all be aiming for a classless society, so I thought, since we're nearly neighbours we could get together some time, maybe swan down to Pleasureland or something. I think you'd get on with me all right as I am brainy and good-looking (tall, slim and blonde with crimson highlights). Also I have high ambitions and am specially gifted. Mrs Crabbe says I have the gift of the Gab, meaning the gift of Gabriel, the angel with the heavenly tongue. How can you resist? You are not so bad-looking yourself, so I won't mind being seen with you.

I look forward to hearing from you.

Best wishes,

Mitzi Puddington.

DEATHWOOD HALL

Walsea

August 6th

Dear Mitzi,

I wasn't really surprised to get your letter as I had quite a bit of female fan-mail after my performance. But I can't get involved with them all, I lead a guarded life as I've had quite a few adventures, including being kidnapped, so my parents keep me on a tight rain. (I expect your brother Colin will have noticed Alex, my father's chuffeur, delivering and collecting me at the stage door.) So I could only pick out one fan for dating and I chose you because I like your name Mitzi, classy with a hint of foreign. I thought it might be Russian till I spotted Puddington!! Anyway, Russian's hardly likely if your dad works for the queen, unless he's a double-agent spy, of course. Does he actually live in the palace? Royal connections are something we have in common as my uncle Gordon has been to two royal weddings, so I don't see why we shouldn't meet. I'm not sure what a classless society is but if it's one of these free-range schools where you can wander about and do as you like, I'm all in favour.

I'm sorry you didn't hear much of the play as I thought it was pretty good. I must say I've been well bitten by this acting bug and would love to be in the next WADS production, 'Royal Romps', but my name isn't on the audition list. I guess that's because the producer, Fenella Mouldsley-Burton – (what a mouthful!) – wasn't too pleased about that stray juggling ball, but that was a chance in a billion, not the sort of thing that would ever happen again. I don't suppose you could get your Colin to put in a word for me?

If so, I think we could really be friends, classless society or not, and I might be able to sneak away next Saturday as my mother is having a coffee morning. Everyone will be far too busy to keep an eye on me, and our new Spanish au pair Pilar, who is supposed to be my constant shadow when I'm at home, sneaks off for an early siesta whenever she gets half a chance. I could manage 11.00 a.m. to about 12.30 so let me know if you are up for it. We could meet in the park. I'll be sitting on the bandstand steps sketching the war memorial. Sketching is another side of my artistic nature and will save me the shame of being seen hanging about like a lost sheep if you are late or stand me up. (Which of course would scupper our friendship before it got started, crimson headlights or not!)

I am glad to note that you are a very good speller, which most of my girl friends are not, so I guess you really are brainy and probably good at Scrabble which is one of my favourite games. So now I am checking all my own spellings very carfully to keep up with you, it won't be time wasted, it will be good for my future career, even if I follow my dad into parliament. (And for a cracking start, I've just checked that 'parliament' has two 'a's in it, though I can't imagine why.) Please don't email me, though. MI5 took to checking my computer when we had this major panic over some missing government documents – (as usual everybody thought I was up to the neck in it which I wasn't) – and I'd hate to think anything so embarrassing might happen again.

Write back soon to your possibly new friend,

Damian

99 Beach Prospect,
Walsea

8th August

Dear Possible Friend Damian,
So you're willing to take a risk on me, are you? In that case, I'll risk a stroll to the bandstand next Saturday morning at 11 a.m. Let's hope the band's not playing that day or the trombone might shoot out and knock you off the steps. I'll be wearing my green top with the diamanté feature and white cut-offs. I might bring a picnic if it's a nice day. My auntie Velda who lives with us has a friend called Jen who works in a pastry-shop. Jen keeps us in leftovers, especially their wiz cheese-and-onion rolls. Two of those and you're ready to shoot the rapids!

In case you're wondering, Auntie Velda lives with us because she got jilted at the altar by Puffing Billy Cutter. It was a mega drama. I was her bridesmaid and as we started up the aisle Billy just took one look at her and fled. He ran out so fast that his special wedding hairpiece flew off and landed in the font. Talk about pandemonium! We've never seen him since but as you can guess, Auntie V is crazy for revenge, and I mean crazy. One day she's going to explode, and murder will be done, you mark my words.

Still, life goes on, and you will be pleased to know I have already asked our Colin to put in a good word for you with bossy old Mouldy-Burger.

I expect you noticed he's nuts about her and is always trying to suck up to her by painting scenery and scouting around for props and bits of costume, etc., so she might do him this favour as a reward. She is far too snobby to actually go out with him (she's just the upper crust sort Mrs Crabbe says is sucking civilisation dry and bringing it to its knees) but our Col, the daft idiot, will never give up hope.

You didn't give me your email address so I couldn't have used it even if I'd wanted to. Anyway, our Colin reads all my emails (it's his computer) so when we're talking personal stuff I prefer a safe, sealed envelope.

You'll notice I haven't even asked for your phone number. That's because I like writing letters, it gives you time to think properly about what you want to say. Phoning is just the opposite, my family does all its arguing, cursing and fighting on the phone. They blurt out rude, rotten things to one another, then are too proud to apologise. You'd be amazed how many lives get ruined this way!

Please note my dad is not a spy, though he has been up to some clever tricks in his time. He's an inventor, one of his most useful was a PIN number storer and selector which would hold over a thousand numbers, only it was a bit too successful and created a lot of jealousy so it got banned. I'm amazed you don't know what 'at Her Majesty's pleasure' means, and you with a dad in parliament. And I'm sorry to disappoint you, but our only royal connection is that my dad's called Albert, same as Queen Victoria's old man. Still, if you're worth knowing, this won't put you off taking that risk on me.

Hoping to see you soon, then!

Your Possible-but-hoping-to-be-Permanent Friend

Mitzi.

DEATHWOOD HALL

Walsea

August 14th

Dear Mitzi,

I like taking risks, it's the best fun I get. I need to break out now and then from being 'detained at my parents' pleasure'. Sometimes it's worth it, sometimes not. That picnic was a risk, in more ways than one! You never said you were bringing your kid sister with you. If I'd known I'd have worn my Uncle Gordon's suit of armour that his ancient four-bear killed three Scots in. Your Suzie is pretty hyper, my left ankle and both shins are black and blue. As these were visible below my shorts our cook, Mrs Harris, wanted to put stuff on them as soon as I got home. She asked what happened so I had to lie and say I got tackled playing soccer (I'm in St Aidan's Academy second eleven, in goal). Luckily she was too busy to go and tell my mother or to remember St A's was closed for the Summer. She is always very 'Harrissed' (joke) and easily forgets things. As for Pilar, our 'au pilar' (second joke!), she didn't even notice I was limping. When she's actually awake she goes about in a permanent Spanish gloom, I guess she's homesick.

I must say I didn't like your auntie Velda's friend Jen's famous rolls much either, especially after your Suzie squeezed dandelion 'gravy' all over them. I took one home and tried it out on our dog Victor but he gave one sniff and stalked away. He's a very aristocratic dog with refined tastes.

So, I have to admit that on the whole it wasn't exactly a five-star date. A good job your Colin sent word he'd fixed my audition for 'Royal Romps', though I don't know what he means about it all depending on a tiara. I've certainly no intention of wearing one, whatever part I get.

By the way, what your brother needs to improve his flagging love affair is an exotic present and I know just the thing. Our new gardener, Will Blades, has begun growing orchids in our greenhouse. He's a proper expert, these are pretty rare and stunning blooms that win competitions. So as a thank-you for your Colin fixing me up, I could sneak one out for him to present to Mouldy-Burger.

As for keeping in touch by phone, I agree about the arguing and cursing, you should hear what goes on at our place. I wouldn't have given you my number anyway, as my father checks all the bills with a magnifying glass and I'm not supposed to be dating girls.

Bruised and battered but still brainstorming,
Your damaged new friend,
Damian.

P.S. I found out 'at Her Majesty's pleasure' means in prison, so what has your dad been up to??? And why was Auntie Velda's bloke called Puffing Billy?

99 Beach Prospect,
Walsea

16th August

Dear Damaged and Disgruntled Damian,
I think you are pretty mean to blame me for what happened on Saturday. I couldn't help bringing our Suzie, I was stuck with her as my mum was at work (you must have seen her, she is Gypsy Gemma reading palms in that jazzy kiosk on the pier and Saturdays are her busiest days) and my auntie Velda, who usually baby-sits, was having one of her turns. It was this pop-star's wedding on the T.V. news that set her off, especially as the bridegroom looked a bit like Puffing Billy. My mum christened him that, by the way, long before the non-wedding, because she said he was all puff and no backbone, not to mention overweight and chugging behind his lawnmower like an old steam train (he's a full-time gardener). I daren't tell you what she calls him now.

Our Col says thanks for the orchid offer, but it won't alter the fact that your part in 'Royal Romps' will depend on you

LENDING them a tiara, (not having to wear one, silly!). He has promised Mouldy faithfully that he can get one, so don't let him down or it will cancel out any good the prize orchid might do. By the way, don't mention orchids in front of Auntie Velda, she had two dozen of them in her redundant wedding bouquet.

Anyway, I am now willing to forgive your complaints and to meet up again, if you can force yourself to keep on dating a jailbird's daughter. (Not that it's MY fault. As Mrs Crabbe says, we don't choose our parents and it's usually best to look elsewhere for guidance – e.g., to HER.) As it happens Dad didn't do anything bad this time, he was a victim, dumped on by one of his so-called pals and wrongly convicted by a gullible, vindictive, hard-hearted judge. He is as innocent as a newborn baby, but boiling up inside like a volcano about to blow. Watch this space!

Yours big-heartedly,

Mitzi.

DEATHWOOD HALL

Walsea

August 18th

Dear Mitzi,

I am not a snob, whatever you think, and I have been mixed up with jailbirds and their families before. Don't forget one of them was well-known to our family but still kidnapped me. Whatever your dad got up to I expect he had his reasons and I am pretty broad-minded. (By the way, at St Aidan's they spell it GAOLbirds, and they are usually right.)

Anyway, I'm the one who should be forgiving YOU, not to mention your Suzie. And please note, my father is NOT a multibillionaire, just an ordinary millionaire which isn't saying much these days, what with Lotto, Bingo, scratch cards and Premium Bonds. He is always hard up and sounding off about the state of the roof and the bills that come in after one of my mother's dinner parties. Still, I have a generous nature and my bruises are starting to fade, so I will say no more about forgiveness and will meet you again after 7.30 p.m. on September 3rd, as that will be the date of the next dinner party. The guest of honour is to be that famous judge who just tried the Ripon Ripper, but that doesn't mean I am on the side of the law. I don't even get to see the guests. As soon as they start arriving I get shunted off to my room where they think I play Scrabble with Pilar, but her English isn't up to it, so actually she's started to teach me Poker instead, which is even better.

Come to think of it, I could teach you Poker if you like, it' s a very exciting game, though it depends a lot on your face. So if you're interested we could fit in an extra meeting at the bandstand on Tues about 3.00 and you could master the basics. It won't cost you anything to start with and I'll bring the orchid, safely nestling in a shoe-box.

Mouldy wanted me to audition for the princess's page boy in Royal Romps, I ask you! No way would I risk such ridicule. I stuck out for Court Jester which has some great laugh-lines to suit my comic talent, and she couldn't very well refuse me when I reminded her that my mother gave WADS a fat donation last time instead of buying tickets and having to sit through it all on those creaky wooden chairs. As nobody else wants to audition for that part – I'm IN! Which means with an adaptable part like that I can easily work in a bit more juggling. That should liven the play up a bit, and from what I've seen of the script it could certainly do with it.

See you for Poker, then.

Cheers, Damian.

99 Beach Prospect

Walsea

August 18th

Dear Jen,

There's no privacy here for phone calls and I want to tell you a secret. I've just found out that Billy Cutter has moved back into the area. You can guess what that's done to me, I've had turn after turn since I found out. My legs have gone to jelly and I can't sleep a wink. It seems he's got the gardener's job at some big house or hotel near here, and when I find out which one it is I'll be in touch pretty darn quick to tell them what he's really like. If he's given them references they'll be fakes and if there are any single women on the premises they need to be warned off. Oooh, I can't wait to let some giant hedge-cutters loose on him and his blasted orchids.

Thanks for the latest batch of cheese and onion rolls, though I can't imagine why you keep making so many if they don't sell. Our Milly, who's hooked on *Hello* magazine and has taken to calling herself Mitzi, snaffled most of them for a picnic with her new boy friend but as far as I know he's still alive.

Get chatting to your customers and see if you can find out where Billy is, then take cover in a bomb-proof shelter.

Love,

Velda

90 Beach Prospect

Walsea

August 18th

Dear Albert,

I'm sorry to say I won't be visiting you this week. Our Colin asked me not to, he wants to have a special chat with you. I offered to come with him but he said no, it has to be private, man-to-man. He was very insistent and I can guess what he's going to talk about. It's that toffee-nosed Fenella Double-barrelled Whatsit from WADS. But you make sure you put him off her, especially if he's talking weddings. I tried myself but he just says oh, stop nagging. He'll take more notice of you. I don't fancy spending the rest of my life being looked down on from a great height and I know you'll feel the same.

We can't wait to have you home, our Milly and Suzie miss you something shocking. I think it's disgusting that you finished up having to mix with all those nasty criminals and I'm worried about that mad look in your eye. Brooding's bad for your stomach and don't forget to take your blood-pressure pills. That Judge Hardman has a lot to answer for, he certainly lives up to his name. If you ask me, he's more of a villain than that Ripon Ripper ever was.

At least you'll be glad to know that all the signs (stars, tarot, crystal, runes and tea-leaves) are favourable for an early release, so for goodness sake keep your nose clean.

Love and kisses,

Your loving wife,

Gemma

Batch the Second

99 Beach Prospect,
Walsea

20th August

Dear Damian,

Sorry I couldn't make it for the Poker lesson after all, our Suzie swallowed a marble and I had to take her to Casualty. Mum was working and it was auntie V's day with her Shrink. (Prof. Eustace Balderdash, a right waste of money and space, but smarmy-charming with it.) Still, I might as well not have bothered. After we'd sat there for nearly two hours the doctor, who looked half dead and couldn't stop yawning, just said not to worry, the marble would roll out in time. I hope you didn't hang about too long. Still, your drawing of the war memorial must be coming on a treat! I guess the orchid will have wilted, but no doubt there'll be plenty more where that came from.

Mrs Crabbe wouldn't have approved of Mouldy being bribed via your wealthy parents' fat donation, just so you could get your own way. Still, you didn't choose your parents either, and in your shoes I'd have done exactly the same.

Guess what, old Mouldy rolled up at Gypsy Gemma's the other day to have her palm read! I'd have thought she'd turn up her snobby nose at mumbo jumbo like that, but apparently she's as superstitious as most feather-brains and was dead keen to know what the future had in store, especially where the next play was concerned. Our Col says she's hungry for fame, obsessed with being a great producer and anxious to be spotted by Hollywood – some hopes! – but I reckon she's just keen to find out if there's a mega-rich upper crust husband waiting in the wings.

My mum is unrecognisable in her gypsy get-up, but she knew who Mouldy was all right and is desperate not to let our Colin get tangled up with the likes of her which would turn us all into doormats for the rest of our lives, especially when she found out where my dad was spending his leisure time. So Mum put her tragic face on and told Mouldy there was a definite blip in her lifeline, an unfortunate major crisis about to happen, something to do with a pushy young man.

'Beware of this young man,' my mum warned, 'otherwise he will bring disaster down upon your head. My advice would be to put him out of your life at once.'

It's all very well for Mum, but our poor Col's going to be devastated, and what's the betting he'll take it out on me?

Write back and console me, and let's fix another meeting sharpish. How about next Tuesday? I can't wait till September 3rd and anyway I want to get cracking on the Poker. If there's money in it, maybe I could spread it round school next term, Mrs Crabbe won't mind, she believes in equal opportunities for all and the re-distribution of wealth.

Your eager friend,

Mitzi.

DEATHWOOD HALL

Walsea

August 23rd

Dear Mitzi,

If your Colin had been going to take it out on you it would have served you right for standing me up. I waited 42 and a half minutes before the Parkie moved me on. I finished sketching the war memorial and gave it a border of wilting orchids as well. But as it happens, you have no need to worry, as I am the one taking all the flak (as usual!). That's because Mouldy decided the pushy young man your mum was going on about must be ME! Your Colin has absolutely no acting talent, as surely you must have noticed, so that ruled HIM out, and now Mouldy thinks *I'm* the unsophisticated trouble in store and has sacked me from 'Royal Romps' with some lame excuse about a shortage of curly-toed shoes my size. Well, they'll be sorry, because now there will be no juggling, which was the highlight of the last production.

So one way and another I am really cheesed off, especially about losing that Court Jester part. We'd already had one awkward misunderstanding at home a while ago, over me not playing the part of Macbeth in a school production, which my folks really DID want to see. Now everybody' s going to start thinking I'm a drama jinx which means I'll never get any parts anywhere. So you jolly well ought to make your Colin persuade his lady-love to put me back in the play. It's the least you can do, as this is all your mum's fault.

I'll see you Tuesday, then, same arrangement, and this time you'd better be there. None of my other girlfriends has ever dared to stand me up.

Your disgruntled friend,

Damian.

P.S. You've had the orchid now; it died a sad and lonely death but is immortalised in my sketch. Our gardener Will noticed it was missing, he went berserk, you'd have thought I'd plucked his right arm off instead of one measly flower, so I daren't steal any more. He treats them like his own flesh and blood. In fact, he thinks more of his blessed orchids than he does of any human being. Even Ricky, his assistant, isn't aloud to touch them.

4, Scaton Walk,
Walsea
24th August

Dear Velda,

I hope you are feeling less wobbly by now. If not, maybe this classy Get Well card (and my news) will cheer you up. I chatted up one of the customers who belongs to a gardening club. He kept nattering on about this Will Blades who gave them a talk about growing prize orchids, and it suddenly dawned on me that it might be your Billy Cutter who's changed his name to Will Blades in hopes of staying incognito. Well, it's worth a try. All you have to do now is to look through the telephone directory for W. Blades, then ring up and that will settle it one way or the other. Best of all, if it is him you'll have found out where he's living.

How's that for a good bit of detective work? It's amazing what you can discover in a busy cake shop, provided you're bright enough to pick up the clues.

And I'm still listening, this could just be the start, so keep your pecker up.

Love,

Jen

99 Beach Prospect,
Walsea

30th August

Dear Damian,

Well, I wouldn't give today more than 3 stars, it's not everybody's cup of tea, sitting in the bandstand in the pouring rain being taught how to play Poker by somebody who keeps criticising your face. I must say you're a better gambler than you are a teacher. My poor old head was spinning by the time we'd finished.

Maybe that was why I had this strange hallucination on my way home. I spotted this bloke lurking about in the shadows round the back of the church and I could have sworn it was my dad. It couldn't have been, of course, because as you know he is otherwise engaged, but it didn't half give me a turn.

Our Colin and Mouldy have had a falling-out and Col says it's because he can't get hold of that blessed tiara, which he promised her faithfully he would. This has depressed him more than a double tax bill. He's moping about, sulking worse than our Suzie and playing depressing music, though that's not a bit like him, he's pretty cheerful and easy-going as a rule. I'm worried all this might stir up the crime that's already lurking in his blood.

I hope you realise this is all your fault. Surely your mum has got a tiara if she's always entertaining bigwigs? Why don't you ask her? You owe our Col for his efforts on your behalf (past and possibly future), and I don't fancy having TWO members of my family detained at Her Majesty's pleasure.

Yours hopefully,

Mitzi.

DEATHWOOD HALL

Walsea

August 31st

Dear Mitzi,

I wish you'd stop going on about that blessed tiara. My mother HASN'T GOT ONE. She used to have lots of jewels, the real McCoy, but they got stolen and as there was some problem with the insurance my father thought she should stick to fakes in future. The fakes do NOT include a tiara, which would be O.T.T. for her kind of party anyway, and even the stuff she has is at the bank. If your Col's so good at scenery and props, surely he could make one out of cardboard, glue and glass beads? He seems to have plenty of time on his hands and theatre people are supposed to use their ingenuity. *Blue Peter* showed how to make one once and it looked okay.

By the way, you'll be interested to know your auntie Velda's Shrink, Eustace BALDERTON (!), is also one of my parents' guests for Sept. 3rd, so I hope Auntie V hasn't mentioned my name to him in one of her heart-to-heart confessionals. Our meetings are supposed to be SECRET, and you never know what he'll blurt out when my father's cocktails get flowing.

I'm really looking forward to Saturday. This time let's meet at the front of the pier. I'll have much more time to spend with you than usual. Our home crowd will be partying until all hours so we must make the most of it. We could go to the Fun Fair and/or the pictures and/or for a good feed. I haven't yet told them at home that I've been sacked from 'Royal Romps' so to get myself out of the house I'm pretending there's an important rehearsal that night. Better still, Alex (my father's chuffeur) has been commandeared to ferry some of the guests, which gets HIM out of the way. Pilar will have to shaperone me by taxi instead, but don't worry, I'll soon get rid of her, she'll be glad of an evening off. She's always grumbling that she hasn't seen any night life since she came to England and is raring to go. I know we could easily walk to the pier, but if we don't leave home in that taxi my mother will start having fits about me being kidnapped again. Once we've dumped her, Pilar won't be left on her own for long, she's the flaunty sort that gets builders and lorry drivers whistling whenever she sashays past.

I must say it's a great relief to have a girlfriend who lives in the same town. It's usually a major operation just getting them over to Walsea, you wouldn't believe the trouble I've had and the time I've wasted. My friend Frankie comes on the bus, and Tracey either bikes or gets dropped off in her dad's van, the timing is a nightmare, so I'm going to make the most of you while I can.

Roll on Saturday!

Cheers, Damian.

Batch the Third

99 Treachery Prospect,
Walsea

Not-so-Dear Damian,
So what happened to you last night the much heralded Third of September? I don't call THAT making the most of me. At least you could have let me know you weren't coming. I stood outside the pier so long I counted 927 cranks of the turnstile. I suppose your family found out and thought I wasn't good enough for you. Mrs Crabbe says titled people are almost as prone as the noovo-rich to have this fatal flaw, which has been the downfall of many a great endeavour.
Well, I am mortally offended, and you'd better have a solid gold excuse for not turning up if you ever want to see me again.

Yours in a mighty huff,

Mitzi.

P.S. Would YOU go to your dad's coronation in a cardboard tiara? Mouldy says only the real thing will do, and quite right too. I wouldn't have thought somebody from a family like yours would need to be told that.

DEATHWOOD HALL

Walsea

Deathwood Crime-scene,

Walsea

September 5th

Dear Mitzi,

As a matter of fact I have a perfect excuse for not turning up on Saturday. Just as I was ready to leave I was grounded. That VIP Judge Hardman that I told you about, who was my parents' guest of honour, actually got bashed over the head in our greenhouse before he'd even had his pre-dinner cocktail. He'd gone to look at Will's wonder orchids and somebody sneaked up and knocked him out cold. Will says this thug just rushed in, attacked from behind and fled before either of them had realised what was happening. I doubt Will would have done much about it anyway. The greenhouse was swimming in blood but he was more concerned about his precious orchids being splashed and damaged.

Talk about chaos! We had paramedics, panicking guests, police with blaring sirens, reporters and photographers popping out of the undergrowth, Mrs Harris's dinner-party nosh all ruined and my mother on the brink of hysteria. Her first thought was that if there was a villain on the premises he must have come to kidnap me again. She reckoned this villain must have hit the judge to get him out of the way, then backed off into the bushes to bide his time. So she whisked me off upstairs and locked me in my room. I couldn't even get hold of Pilar to tell her the jaunt was off. But don't waste any sympathy on her, the taxi had been ordered so she just went off in it herself. Had a whale of a time, by all accounts. It's livened her up no end. She's not had one siesta since, and has taken to singing endless Spanish love songs at the top of her screechy voice.

Needless to say, my parents are devastated that a tragedy like this should happen to their guest of honour. My dad says he'll never live it down, it will be splashed all over the front pages for days, and bang go his chances of a cabinet post, even supposing he manages to keep his seat in parliament. Also he reckons it will be a black day for us if any of us ever end up in court now; that law lot stick closer together than gunge on a glue-pot.

So much, as they say, for the best laid plans of mice and men, not that I reckon mice are much good at planning, the rate they finish up in traps.

Cheerless Cheers,

Damian.

4, Scaton Walk,

Walsea

Sept. 5th

Dear Velda,

So that Will Blades was your Billy after all. I knew it! Well, you didn't waste much time, nor let your jelly legs hold you back, I see! Good try, old girl, I didn't think you had it in you, but a pity it didn't work out. I nearly had a fit when I saw it splashed all over the front pages. Thank goodness none of them mentioned your name, so I guess you've not been arrested yet. (When you are, all you have to do is to plead self-defence.) The police are keeping very quiet. If they do know anything they're not naming any names. I bought three different papers, but I couldn't find even the smallest hint that you were mixed up in it, so at least you got something right. But fancy you coming so close to Billy and then hitting the wrong bloke! What happened? Did Billy dodge away at the last minute, or did you just misJUDGE (!) the blow? Or was it just that the other chap realised what you were up to and tried to stop you? It was really bad luck that somebody else was there, and him a law-man. Let's hope that if you DO get found out he's not the one who tries your case! By the way, isn't he the same judge who tried your Albert?

I expect you're pretty fed up that it's all gone wrong, but look on the bright side, at least you've tracked Billy down and found a way to get at him, so you can try again while your blood's Up, and catch him on his own next time.

Never say die – except to Billy!

Love,

Jen

99 Beach Prospect

Walsea

Sept. 4th

Dear Peelar (Pillar?)

Just a quick note to go with this earring I'm returning, which I found after you'd left me last night. It must have dropped into my pocket. I hope the big-wigs don't open staff's letters so it reaches you okay. Lucky you didn't lose it and spoil a pair.

Lucky for me, too, that I bumped into you getting out of that taxi on the prom, and that we had such a wicked time afterwards. I'm hoping that was the first of many as I've now realised my last girl friend was a slave-driving, obsessive drama queen with no finer feelings or sense of humour, and more stuck-up than a roll of fly-paper. You actually saved my life as I was so depressed I was thinking of jumping off the end of the pier and I can't swim! So we absolutely must meet again. You have my mobile number – I wrote it on the back of your hand, remember? – so let me know when you can get away.

Yours affectionately,

Colin xxxxx

99 Beach Prospect

Walsea

Sept. 7th

Dear Jen,

What are you rambling on about? I haven't done anything to Billy, chance would be a fine thing, I didn't even manage to track him down. There was only one W. Blades in the directory and I rang but she was a woman. As for last Saturday night, I never went out. Our Gemma was upset about some gloomy portent she reckoned was hanging over us so I stayed in to keep her company. I guess all this doom and gloom sprang from Albert telling her not to visit for a while as he was in quarantine in the sick bay with something catching. (I'll bet!) But she's also worried about our Colin. That boy's got some sort of a secret and I'm beginning to wonder if it's to do with his dad. He went to see him the other day and he's not been the same since. The last couple of nights he's rolled in late and slept till afternoon. Burglars' hours I call them, so it looks as though he might be following in his dad's footsteps after all, though he hasn't got Albert's inventive flair, more's the pity. Up to now he's always seemed a decent lad, more interested in acting than crime. A pity he can't get a proper job instead of hanging around that so-called theatre, hoping to turn into the next George Clooney.

Needless to say, I'm dying to hear a proper tale about what's been going on with Billy Cutter. Our Gemma's too cocky to buy newspapers, she thinks she can find out all she needs to know in the stars and tea-leaves, etc.. So please send me the cuttings, then I can see what's what and really get to work on my raging revenge. Prof says I need to get it all out of my system.

Love,

Velda.

7 Septiembre

Querido Colleen,

I washing my hands so is gone your nombre.

Muchas gracias for ear ring I thinking I lost through floor of pier. Colleen, I dreaming of you perpetuamente. Can meeting you 2 dias, again the pier?

Is no need atormentar (worry?) of la tiara, I can find and will bringing.

Su amiga

Pilar

99 Tragedy Terrace,
Walsea

7th September

Dear Damian,

Well, it's all happening here. Our Suzie's disappeared and my mum's going frantic. Su was supposed to be playing in the back garden all morning with Auntie V keeping an eye on her. But when Mum came home at lunch time the kid wasn't there. I'd had my earphones on most of the time so I didn't hear anything outside or notice anything wrong, so you can guess how that makes me feel now, not that it's really my fault. Honestly, Auntie V's a dead loss. No wonder Billy took one look at her plodding up the aisle and decided to flee. Mum and V have gone out searching but I've been told to stop here in case Suzie comes back or somebody rings with news.

As if all this isn't enough, I heard about that carry-on with your judge, and now you tell me he was Judge Hardman, the low-life who put my dad away. Why didn't you say it was him in the first place? You just said he was the Ripon

Ripper bloke, and I didn't connect the two. So now I'm wondering whether that really was my dad I saw the other day. If he'd found out the judge was coming here he could have escaped and struck the blow, he's been boiling up for it long enough. Mrs Crabbe says sometimes violence is the only way to bring justice to the oppressed. Still, I'm praying it was one of your other guests, there must be loads of folks who hate all judges and that one in particular. Talking of guests, didn't I hear that the Home Secretary once got done at your place? I must say your family's very careless with its visitors. I thought your Victor was supposed to be a guard dog.

Looks like we could have done with a guard dog here, it would have been more use than Auntie V.

Your frantic friend,

Mitzi.

DEATHWOOD HALL

Walsea

September 9th

Dear Mitzi,

Don't worry, if your dad had escaped it would have been in all the papers and the police would have been round to yours, emptying cupboards and pulling the floorboards up.

Sorry to hear about your Suzie but I'm sure she'll turn up, no kidnapper in his right mind would want to hang on to her for long, and if it's any comfort you're not the only one with troubles.

We've got MI5 here again, which means goodbye to privacy and hello to nervous breakdowns. Judge H. is still unconscious in Intensive Care and his bodyguard, who was chatting up one of the temporary kitchen staff at the time of the attack, has got the sack. I expect he feels even worse than you do.

Then Pilar disappeared, but it turned out she'd been arrested for shoplifting at that big, posh jeweller's in the High Street. Their floor-walker stopped her at the door trying to sneak out with a TIARA in her bag – how's that for a strange turn of fate? She'd been trying some on in the shop, saying she was about to be invited to a royal reception, but when the police arrived she changed her tale to some wild rubbish about her boyfriend needing the tiara to stop him jumping off the pier when he couldn't swim. She hasn't even got a boyfriend over here. I didn't think she had that much imagination, but these Spaniards are a very highly strung lot. She got off with a caution as it was her first offence and she flashed her eyelashes, etc., at the cops, but all the same my mother says she will have to go, we can't employ staff with criminal tendencies. (And I can guess what your bolshie Mrs Crabbe would think about that, so don't bother telling me.)

School starts again on the 12th so I'm feeling pretty low, can't even get in a game of Poker now. For goodness sake cheer me up.

Yours,

Damian.

P.S. How old are you? Maybe you could apply for Pilar's job.

99 Beach Madhouse,
Walsea

Sept. 9th

Dear Damian,
I'd just sealed your last letter when they found our Suzie. She says her daddy came and took her to Macdonald's for lunch, but Mum found her toddling along the High Street on her own. That kid's a right little romancer. Mum's now quizzing her like the Spanish Inquisition, trying to get to the bottom of it and Auntie V's busy having another turn as camouflage so we can't turn on her. My guess is, young Suzie just fancied an adventure as we all do at times, though she knows she's not supposed to wander off on her own, the little horror. You are so lucky to be an only child.
Can't get away for a bit. I'm stuck with Suzie now and she's not allowed further than the garden gate.
Here's to better times!

Cheers,

Mitzi.

P.S. You should never ask a lady her age. Anyway, I wouldn't dream of being your au pair, I have much loftier ambitions, as I am sure I already told you. Anyway, Mrs Crabbe reckons it's obscene for one person to wait on and clean up after another, unless they're nursing the sick.

DEATHWOOD HALL

Walsea

Ms Velda Puddington,

99 Beach Prospect, Walsea

9th September

Dear Ms Puddington,

Thank you for your many telephone and written messages. We appreciate your concern about our gardening staff but can assure you that Mr Blades came to us with impeccable references and we have so far had no cause for complaint.

You have done your duty as you saw it, so your conscience is now clear and you may spare yourself the inconvenience and expense of contacting us further.

Yours sincerely,

Amanda Drake

99 Beach Bonanza
Walsea

Sept. 10

Dear Damian,

Guess what, my dad's come home! He wasn't expected for ages yet, but he hasn't escaped, it turns out he got tagged for early release just after our Colin had been to see him. He didn't let on to any of us, though, as he was hatching a wicked plan. He stayed with his friend Oscar for the first few nights because he reckoned he'd soon be on his way back to jail and didn't want us mixed up in it.

Our Colin had realised who your Ripon Ripper judge was and went to tell Dad that Hardman was coming to dinner at your place. So Dad, being mad for revenge, decided this was the perfect opportunity to do Hardman over while he was relaxed and off guard. He told Col that another stretch would be worth it for the satisfaction of beating the dust out of the old boy's pants. But as it turned out he was too late, somebody had got there before him. Just as Dad reached your gates clutching our Col's baseball bat, the judge was already being carted off on a stretcher.

So then Dad wanted to come home after all, but he was a bit wary; he didn't know how we'd take it when we found out what he'd been meaning to do. So he nobbled our Suzie first, primed her, then sent her home to break the news. Mum said how irresponsible could you get, letting a four-year-old loose on the town, but he swore he wasn't far behind the kid, watching her all the way until she met up safely with Mum. In the end he realised we must not have believed her, so he just turned up anyway.

As you can imagine, Mum was gob-smacked, Auntie V had a double turn and Suzie kept yelling, 'I told you I'd seen my daddy, didn't I? Didn't I tell you I'd seen him?' I had to shut her in the spare back bedroom. Still, all's well that ends well, Mum's turned all-forgiving and Dad's promised to go straight now, at least until his tag comes off.

I bet you can't beat that for exciting news.

Your sizzling friend,

Mitzi.

P.S. I've just heard we're having a welcome-home party for Dad next Saturday so I hope you can come. (You'd better!) Our Col says you definitely ought to bring Pilar as well, in case you get kidnapped again, so I hope she hasn't gone home yet.

DEATHWOOD HALL

Walsea

Deathwood Drama Hall,

Walsea

September 12th

Dear Mitzi,

Oh, yes, I can beat you for exciting news! Wait till you see the papers tomorrow! Victor and I are heroes, we found the g.b.h. weapon – bloodstained pruning shears berried in the garden with some of the judge's hairs stuck to them. I was playing a game with Victor when he dug them up, and with my experience of top-level crime I realised right away what we'd stumbled on to. The press took photos of us neatly posed outside the notorious taped-up greenhouse (near where we found the weapon) with a background of orchids blooming through the glass. It will be on all the front pages. A good thing I'm used to fame and won't let it go to my head.

Thanks to our brilliance, the police have now made an arrest right here at ours. And what a surprise, the villain who clobbered old Hardman had been on the premises all the time. You'll never guess who it was – none other than